JUL   2014

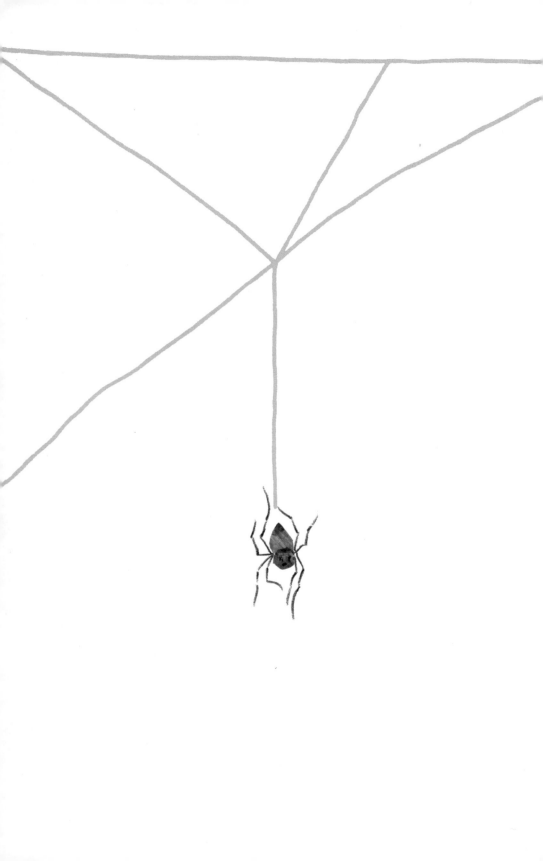

Dear Parents and Educators,

Welcome to Penguin Young Readers! As parents and educators, you know that each child develops at his or her own pace—in terms of speech, critical thinking, and, of course, reading. Penguin Young Readers recognizes this fact. As a result, each Penguin Young Readers book is assigned a traditional easy-to-read level (1–4) as well as a Guided Reading Level (A–P). Both of these systems will help you choose the right book for your child. Please refer to the back of each book for specific leveling information. Penguin Young Readers features esteemed authors and illustrators, stories about favorite characters, fascinating nonfiction, and more!

The Very Busy Spider

LEVEL **2**

GUIDED READING LEVEL **I**

This book is perfect for a **Progressing Reader** who:
- can figure out unknown words by using picture and context clues;
- can recognize beginning, middle, and ending sounds;
- can make and confirm predictions about what will happen in the text; and
- can distinguish between fiction and nonfiction.

Here are some **activities** you can do during and after reading this book:
- Make Predictions: Pretend it is another day and the spider is spinning another web. What other animals come to her? What noises do they make? How do they try to distract her? What does the spider tell them?
- Creative Writing: Work with the child to write a paragraph about a time he/she was very focused on accomplishing a project. Did anyone try to distract him/her? How did he/she remain focused?

Remember, sharing the love of reading with a child is the best gift you can give!

—Bonnie Bader, EdM
Penguin Young Readers program

*Penguin Young Readers are leveled by independent reviewers applying the standards developed by Irene Fountas and Gay Su Pinnell in *Matching Books to Readers: Using Leveled Books in Guided Reading*, Heinemann, 1999.

For Bill and Phyllis

PENGUIN YOUNG READERS
Published by the Penguin Group
Penguin Group (USA) LLC, 375 Hudson Street, New York, New York 10014, USA

USA | Canada | UK | Ireland | Australia | New Zealand | India | South Africa | China

penguin.com
A Penguin Random House Company

The Library of Congress has cataloged the Philomel edition
under the following Control Number: 84005907

ISBN 978-0-448-48052-7 (pbk)   10 9 8 7 6 5 4 3 2
ISBN 978-0-448-48053-4 (hc)   10 9 8 7 6 5 4 3 2 1

The Very Busy Spider

by Eric Carle

Penguin Young Readers
An Imprint of Penguin Group (USA) LLC

Early one morning, the wind blew
a spider across the field.
A thin, silky thread trailed from
her body.

The spider landed on a fence post
near a farmyard and began to
spin a web with her silky thread.

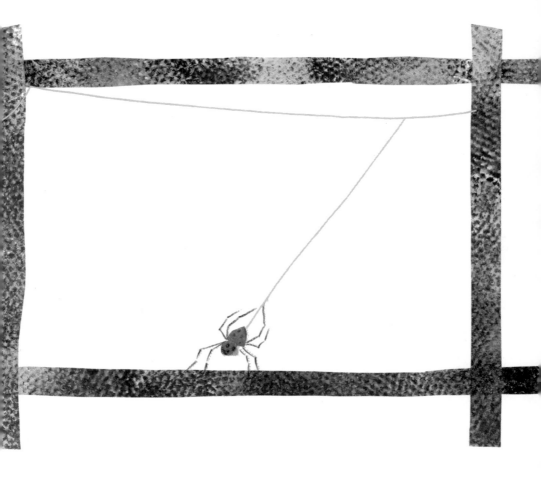

"Neigh! Neigh!" said the horse.

"Want to go for a ride?"

The spider didn't answer.

She was very busy spinning her web.

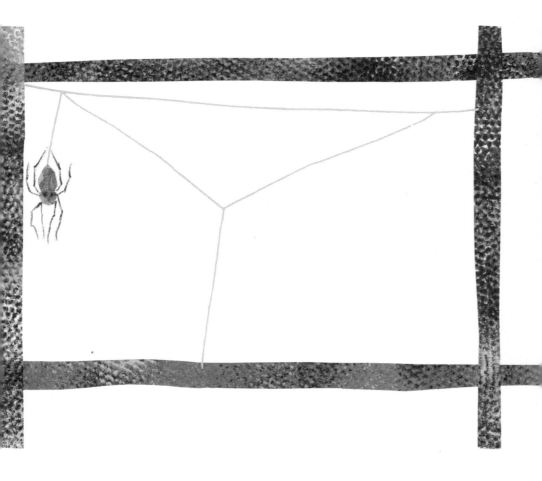

"Moo! Moo!" said the cow.

"Want to eat some grass?"

The spider didn't answer.

She was very busy spinning her web.

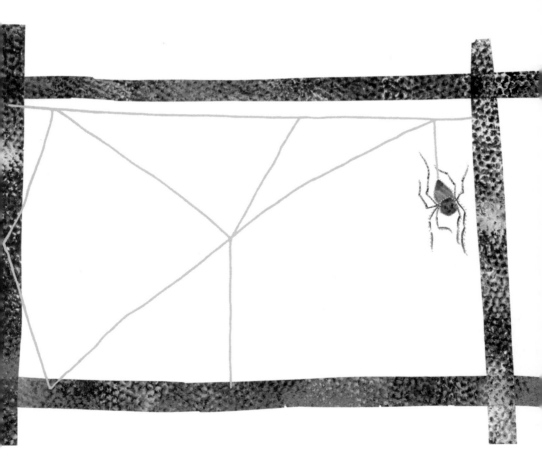

"Bah! Bah!" bleated the sheep.

"Want to run in the meadow?"

The spider didn't answer.

She was very busy spinning her web.

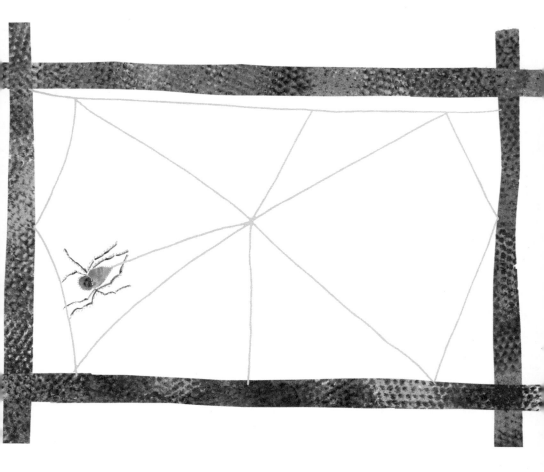

"Maa! Maa!" said the goat.

"Want to jump on the rocks?"

The spider didn't answer.

She was very busy spinning her web.

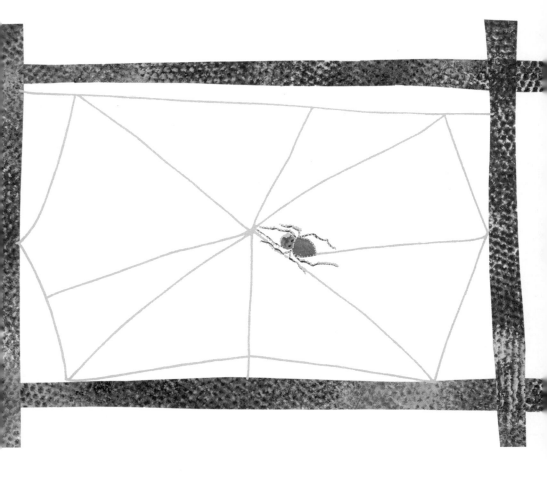

"Oink! Oink!" grunted the pig.

"Want to roll in the mud?"

The spider didn't answer.

She was very busy spinning her web.

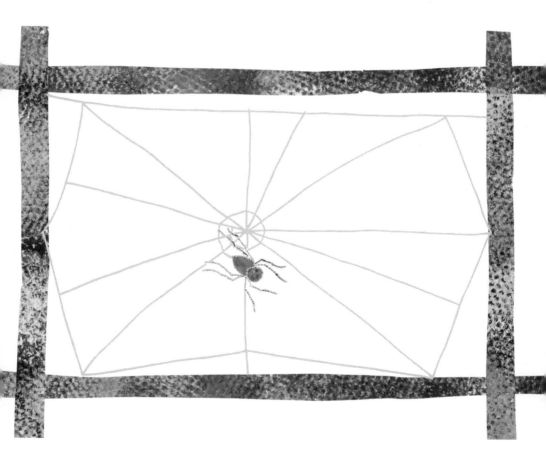

"Woof! Woof!" barked the dog.

"Want to chase a cat?"

The spider didn't answer.

She was very busy spinning her web.

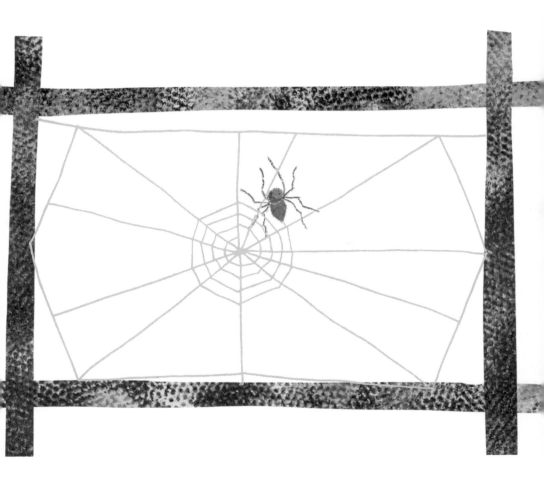

"Meow! Meow!" cried the cat.

"Want to take a nap?"

The spider didn't answer.

She was very busy spinning her web.

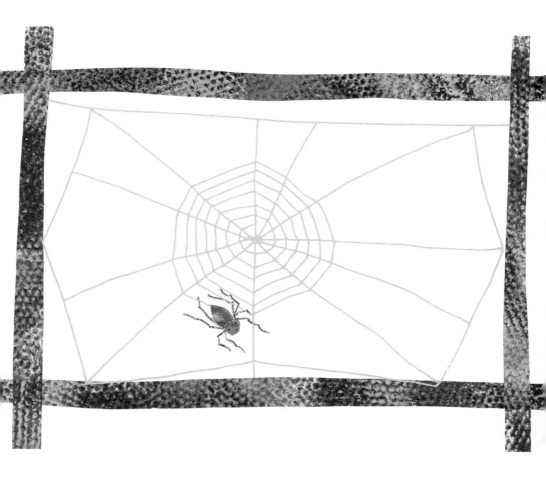

"Quack! Quack!" called the duck.

"Want to go for a swim?"

The spider didn't answer.

She had now finished her web.

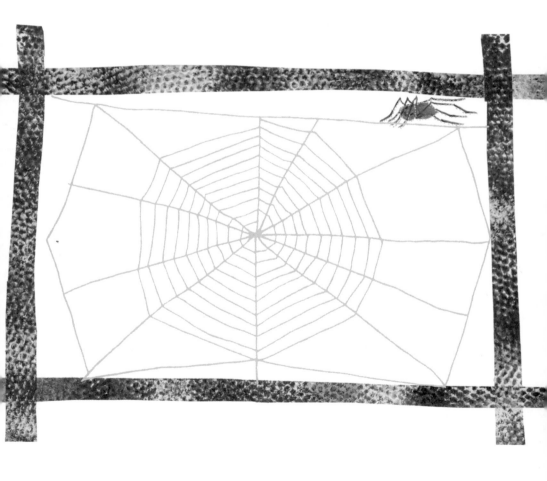

"Cock-a-doodle-do!"

crowed the rooster.

"Want to catch a pesty fly?"

And the spider caught the fly in
her web . . . just like that!

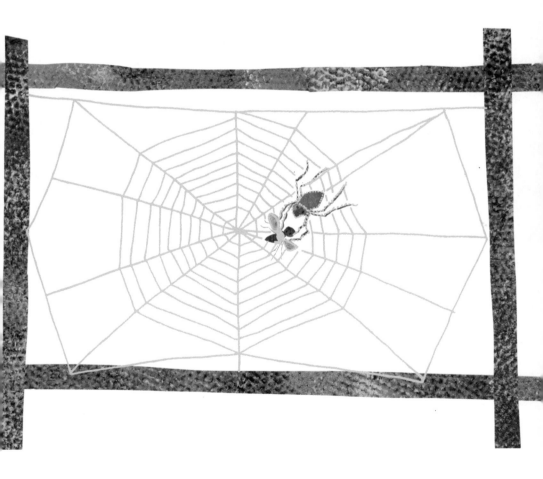

"Whoo? Whoo?" asked the owl.

"Who built this beautiful web?"

The spider didn't answer.

She had fallen asleep.

It had been a very, very busy day.